Dear Parents and Educators,

Welcome to Penguin Young Readers! As parents and educators, you know that each child develops at his or her own pace—in terms of speech, critical thinking, and, of course, reading. Penguin Young Readers recognizes this fact. As a result, each Penguin Young Readers book is assigned a traditional easy-to-read level (1–4) as well as a Guided Reading Level (A–P). Both of these systems will help you choose the right book for your child. Please refer to the back of each book for specific leveling information. Penguin Young Readers features esteemed authors and illustrators, stories about favorite characters, fascinating nonfiction, and more!

Young Cam Jansen and the Knock, Knock Myster[y]

LEVEL **3**

GUIDED READING LEVEL **J**

This book is perfect for a **Transitional Reader** who:
- can read multisyllable and compound words;
- can read words with prefixes and suffixes;
- is able to identify story elements (beginning, middle, end, plot, setting, characters, problem, solution); and
- can understand different points of view.

Here are some **activities** you can do during and after reading this book:
- Summarize: Work with the child to write a short summary about what happened in the story. What happened in the beginning? What happened in the middle? What happened at the end?
- Story Map: Once you have written a short summary, create a story map of *Young Cam Jansen and the Knock, Knock Mystery*. A story map is a visual organizer. The map should include: setting (where and when each story takes place); characters (who is in the story); problem (the difficulty or problem in this story); goal (what the characters want to happen); events (list three things that happened in the story that helped the characters reach their goal); ending (the solution—how the characters solved the problem and achieved their goal).

Remember, sharing the love of reading with a child is the best gift you can give!

—Bonnie Bader, EdM
  Penguin Young Readers program

*Penguin Young Readers are leveled by independent reviewers applying the standards developed by Irene Fountas and Gay Su Pinnell in *Matching Books to Readers: Using Leveled Books in Guided Reading*, Heinemann, 1999.

For my grandsons,
Jacob, Yoni, Andrew, and Aaron—DAA

For Diana, Greg, Hannah Rose,
Mason, and Oliver—SN

PENGUIN YOUNG READERS
Published by the Penguin Group
Penguin Group (USA) LLC, 375 Hudson Street, New York, New York 10014, USA

USA | Canada | UK | Ireland | Australia | New Zealand | India | South Africa | China

penguin.com
A Penguin Random House Company

Text copyright © 2014 by David Adler. Illustrations copyright © 2014 by Susanna Natti.
All rights reserved. Previously published in hardcover in 2014 by Penguin Young Readers.
This paperback edition published in 2015 by Penguin Young Readers, an imprint of
Penguin Group (USA) LLC, 345 Hudson Street, New York, New York 10014. Manufactured in China.

Library of Congress Control Number: 2013027008

ISBN 978-0-14-242225-0   10 9 8 7 6 5 4 3 2 1

Young Cam Jansen
and the Knock, Knock Mystery

by David A. Adler
illustrated by Susanna Natti

Penguin Young Readers
An Imprint of Penguin Group (USA) LLC

Contents

Chapter 1
Sleepy Grandpa Max

"Yummy," Eric Shelton said.
"Grandpa Max bakes
the best cookies."
Eric closed his eyes.
"His cookies have jelly in the middle
and sprinkles on top."
Eric and his friend Cam Jansen
were on their way to visit
Eric's grandparents.

The traffic light was red.

Mrs. Shelton stopped the car.

"We're almost there," she said.

"Their new house

is just two blocks away."

Eric asked Cam, "Do you remember

my grandma and grandpa?"

Cam closed her eyes.

She said, *"Click!"*

Cam always closes her eyes and

says, *"Click!"* when she wants to

remember something.

"I saw them at your birthday party,"

Cam said with her eyes still closed.

"Your grandmother wore a blue

sweater and a purple bead necklace.

Your grandfather wore
a yellow baseball cap."

Cam has an amazing memory.

"My head is filled with pictures,"
Cam says.

"It's like I have a camera in my head.

Click! is the sound my camera makes."

Her parents named her Jennifer.

People found out

about her amazing memory

and called her "the Camera."

Soon "the Camera"

became just "Cam."

The traffic light changed to green.

Eric's mother drove ahead.

"There's Grandpa Max,"

Eric shouted.

Cam opened her eyes.

Eric's grandfather was sitting

on the front porch

of a small red house.

He was sitting in a rocking chair.

He was sleeping.

Chapter 2
Knock! Knock!

Some of the stone blocks
of the front walk were broken.
Fallen branches and apples
were on the walk.
"Be careful," Mrs. Shelton told Cam
and Eric.
"And be quiet," Eric said.
"Grandpa Max is sleeping."
Cam, Eric, and Mrs. Shelton
walked quietly past Grandpa Max.

Mrs. Shelton opened the front door.

Creak!

Grandpa Max opened his eyes.

"I'm not sleeping," he said.

"I'm just resting."

Cam, Eric, and Mrs. Shelton

followed Grandpa Max

into the house.

On a small table in the front room

was a big plate of cookies.

Eric's grandmother was there, too.

In her hand was a large cookie.

And she was sleeping.

"Why are you and Grandma

so tired?" Mrs. Shelton whispered.

"It's the knocking," Grandpa said.

"At night, when we're asleep,

someone knocks on our door.

We get up and answer it,

but no one is there.

We nap during the day,

and someone knocks on our door.

We open the door,

and no one is there."

Cam, Eric, and Mrs. Shelton

sat in the front room.

Eric bit into a cookie.

Sprinkles dropped to the floor.

"Yummy!" Eric said.

"Sh!" Grandpa told him.

"Grandma is sleeping."

"Yummy!" Eric whispered.

Knock! Knock!

Grandma opened her eyes.

"Quick!" she said.

"See who is knocking."

Cam, Eric, and Mrs. Shelton
ran to the front door.
They opened it and looked out.
No one was there.

Chapter 3
"Woo! Woo!"

"Woo! Woo!" Eric said.

"Maybe it's a ghost.

Maybe it's a Knock, Knock Ghost."

"Let's look," Cam said.

There was no ghost hiding

behind Mrs. Shelton's car.

There was no ghost under it.

There was no ghost behind

the apple tree.

Eric said, "Maybe the Knock, Knock
Ghost is hiding in the back."
Cam, Eric, and Mrs. Shelton
went to the backyard.
There was no ghost
hiding behind the fence.
There was no ghost
behind the apple tree.

"We should hide here," Cam said.
"From here, we can see
who is knocking."
Cam and Eric hid behind the tree.
Eric's mother went into the house
to visit with Grandma and Grandpa.
Cam and Eric looked and waited.
"This is boring," Eric said.

"Let's play a memory game."

Cam closed her eyes.

"What am I wearing?" Eric asked.

Just then Mrs. Shelton

hurried outside.

"Did you catch the ghost?"

she asked.

Cam opened her eyes.

"Did you catch whoever just knocked on Grandma and Grandpa's door?"

Chapter 4
Cam Ran to Eric;
Eric Ran to Cam

"We didn't catch anyone,"

Eric told his mother.

"We were playing a memory game."

"Was the knock on the front door

or the back door?" Cam asked.

"I don't know," Mrs. Shelton said.

"Grandma and Grandpa

were resting.

Then 'Knock! Knock! Knock!'

Those knocks woke them."

Cam told Eric,

"Let's go inside.

I'll wait by the front door.

You'll wait by the back door.

As soon as there is a knock,

we'll open the door

and see who it is."

Cam sat by the front door.

Eric sat by the back door.

Cam and Eric waited.

Then it happened.

Knock! Knock!

Cam ran to Eric.

Eric ran to Cam.

Cam told Eric,

"There was no knock

at the front door."

Eric told Cam,

"There was no knock

at the back door."

Cam thought for a moment.

She closed her eyes and said, *"Click!"*

Cam looked at the picture

of the front walk

she had in her head.

"That's it!" Cam said.

She opened her eyes and said,

"I know what's making

those knock, knock sounds."

Chapter 5
No More Knock, Knocks!

Cam said to Mrs. Shelton,
"You told us to be careful
when we got out of your car."
"I didn't want you to fall,"
Mrs. Shelton said.
"Some of the stone blocks
of the front walk are broken.
There are also branches
and apples on the walk."

Cam said, "Those apples
fell from the trees
in the front and back of the house.
When they fell,
some of them hit the roof
and made the knock, knock sounds."

Cam, Eric, and Mrs. Shelton
walked outside.
They looked up at the apple trees.
Mrs. Shelton said, "There are still
lots of apples on the trees.

The apples will keep falling
and keep waking Grandma
and Grandpa."
"They won't fall,
if we pick them," Eric said.
Mrs. Shelton got a ladder
from the garage.
Cam and Eric took turns
climbing the ladder.

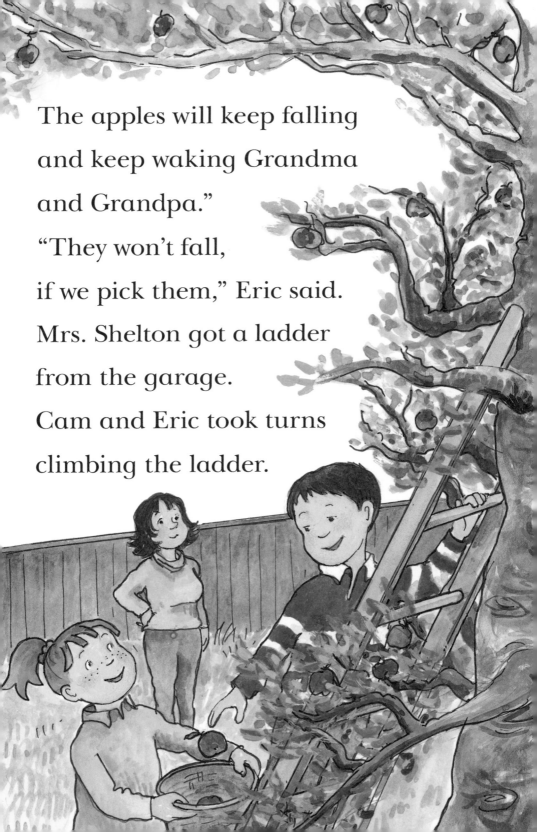

They picked all the apples.

That afternoon,

Cam, Eric, Mrs. Shelton,

Grandma, and Grandpa

baked apple pies, apple tarts, and

apple cookies.

They made applesauce.
That night there were lots of
apple treats for dessert.
That night there was no
Knock, Knock Ghost.

A Cam Jansen Memory Game

Take another look at the picture on page 30.
Study it.
Blink your eyes and say, "Click!"
Then turn back to this page
and answer these questions:

1. How many people are in the picture?

2. Who is peeling an apple?

3. Who is mixing dough?

4. Who is holding a hot apple pie?

5. Is there a rolling pin on the table?

6. What color is Cam's shirt?